All Safe
in the Stable

Dedications

MH to Mike and SS to Ann

2013

D1307052

UK   ISBN-13: 978-1-85985-571-7
        ISBN-10: 1-85985-571-7

USA ISBN-13: 978-0-8254-7305-5
        ISBN-10: 0-8254-7305-5

Distributed in the UK by Marson Book Services Ltd,
PO Box 269, Abingdon, Oxon OX14 4YN

Distributed in the USA by Kregel Publications,
Grand Rapids, Michigan 49501

Worldwide co-edition produced by Lion Hudson plc, Mayfield
House, 256 Banbury Road, Oxford OX2 7DH
Tel: +44 (0) 1865 302750 Fax: +44 (0) 1865 302757
Email: coed@lionhudson.com
www.lionhudson.com

Printed in Singapore

**The story of the first Christmas can be found
in Luke chapters 1 and 2.**

All Safe
in the Stable

by Mig Holder

Illustrated by Steve Smallman

CANDLE
BOOKS

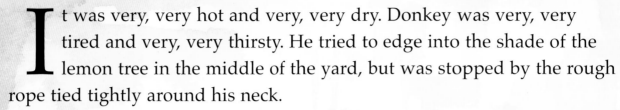

It was very, very hot and very, very dry. Donkey was very, very tired and very, very thirsty. He tried to edge into the shade of the lemon tree in the middle of the yard, but was stopped by the rough rope tied tightly around his neck.

His fur itched, and irritating little flies buzzed around his face and bit into his sore skin. Even when he flicked his long ears to frighten them off, it didn't seem to make any difference. He had never, ever felt so miserable.

All the other animals had long gone except for Rat, who was scurrying about picking up bits of food left in the dirt.

There were just a couple
of men talking in the marketplace
in the middle of this long, hot day.

"Nobody interested in *you* then?" asked Rat.

Donkey snorted loudly but didn't answer.

Suddenly he pricked up his long ears. The two men were talking about *him*. He recognised the voice of his owner.

"Oh yes, he's a lovely runner."

The other, younger man sounded doubtful. "Is this the only one you've got left?"

"'Fraid so – there's been a big run on donkeys this week. Everyone seems to be on the move."

"Tell me about it," said the younger man. "We don't want to go either. D'you think this bag of bones would *make* it as far as Bethlehem?"

Bag of bones, indeed! Donkey was getting really angry now.

"No problem," came back the oily voice of his owner. "Tell you what, I'll chuck in a bag of hay for good measure."

Donkey heard the chinking of coins changing hands. The younger man must have decided to buy him.

Now his owner was speaking again. "And if it won't start in the morning, just give it a good kick."

That was it.

"I'm a '*he*' not an '*it*'," muttered Donkey to himself. "I'll show him who can kick!"

And as his new owner untied the rope from the ring on the wall and tugged him forwards, Donkey bucked and kicked out his back hooves at the cruel man who had hurt him for so long.

The man fell headlong, spilling his money and yelling at the top of his voice. But Donkey didn't so much as glance behind him as his new owner tied the bundle of hay across his back and led him off by the rope around his neck.

It was almost dark when they arrived. Donkey was so tired
he could hardly lift his hooves. They stopped in a yard
surrounded by huts and sheds, tools and piles of wood.
People were tidying up at the end of the day and
a straggle of children ran out to meet them.
A young woman appeared from a doorway
and hurried across. She looked excited.

"Oh Joseph, you got one!"

(So that was his new owner's
name – Joseph.)

Then her face fell; she looked
Donkey up and down.

"Is *that* all you could find?"

Donkey's poor, tired head
drooped and his heart
sank even lower.
Nobody liked him
at all.

Then, unexpectedly, the young woman laughed and patted him on the back. She bent over to look Donkey in the eye. "Don't look so sad," she said. "Things aren't that bad."

Joseph laughed, "Now don't start getting fond of it, Mary – it's not a pet!" And with that, he tugged Donkey into a shed, threw down some straw and shut the door.

"Looks like things have gone from bad to worse," said a small sharp voice.

Donkey peered about in the gloom, but there was nothing there except a leather bucket half-full of water.

"I'm over here," came the same sharp voice again.

At last Donkey made out a small figure lounging in the hay.

"Rat!" exclaimed Donkey. "What are you doing here?"

"Oh, I just came along for the ride," drawled Rat.

"Ride?" Donkey was puzzled.

Rat pointed his sharp nose towards the bale of hay that had been strapped across Donkey's back. Donkey had a little smile at this. "You *didn't*! But how did you get in there?"

Rat made a face. "Easy – I just climbed in when no one was looking."

"But I thought you hated People?"

Rat just shrugged. "I can always disappear again – whenever I want." Then he said, more kindly, "Tell you what, why don't you and I make a break for it and find our own way in the world?"

At this, Donkey's misery washed over him again. He nudged at the rope around his neck, "How can I?" Rat was right. He had to go wherever People dragged him. Was this owner going to be any better than the last one? What lay in store for him? He would soon find out…

It didn't seem as if Donkey had been asleep for a minute when the shed door scraped open and Joseph stood there, outlined against the moonlit sky. It wasn't even morning yet!

"Come on!" said Joseph, pulling Donkey to his feet. "We must make an early start." He grabbed Donkey's rope, pulled him out into the yard, and began loading him up with all sorts of things – pots and pans, blankets, leather water-bottles, and two big baskets filled with fruit, nuts, and bread, one hanging on each side of Donkey's back.

It was all so heavy that Donkey's poor knees began to buckle under him. He looked around for his only friend – but Rat was nowhere to be seen.

As Joseph began to lead him out of the yard, Donkey realised that there was worse to come. The young woman came lumbering out of the house carrying yet another bundle of clothes. Then she climbed on his back, too!

"You might as well," said Joseph. "You're going to be tired enough as it is."

Tired! It's all right for her – what about me! thought Donkey, as Joseph slapped him on the back to make him start walking.

It was only just beginning to get light and the air was still cool. But, as they trudged along and the sun began to climb in the sky, the path ahead became steeper and steeper, and Donkey became hotter and hotter and crosser and crosser.

Why do I have to do this? he thought, *I'm tired of doing what People tell me.* Then he stopped. He just stopped.

Maybe Rat was right; I should have run away.

Joseph pulled him. Joseph pushed him. Joseph shouted at him. But still Donkey would not move. Joseph was running out of patience.

Then Mary had an idea.

"I'll get off and walk," she said, climbing off Donkey's back and patting him on his neck. "Poor old thing! You look exhausted already."

Donkey couldn't believe his ears – *Poor thing?* No one had ever thought about his feelings before!

So the three of them trudged in silence up the steep path, down the next and up the next, getting slower and slower the steeper it became.

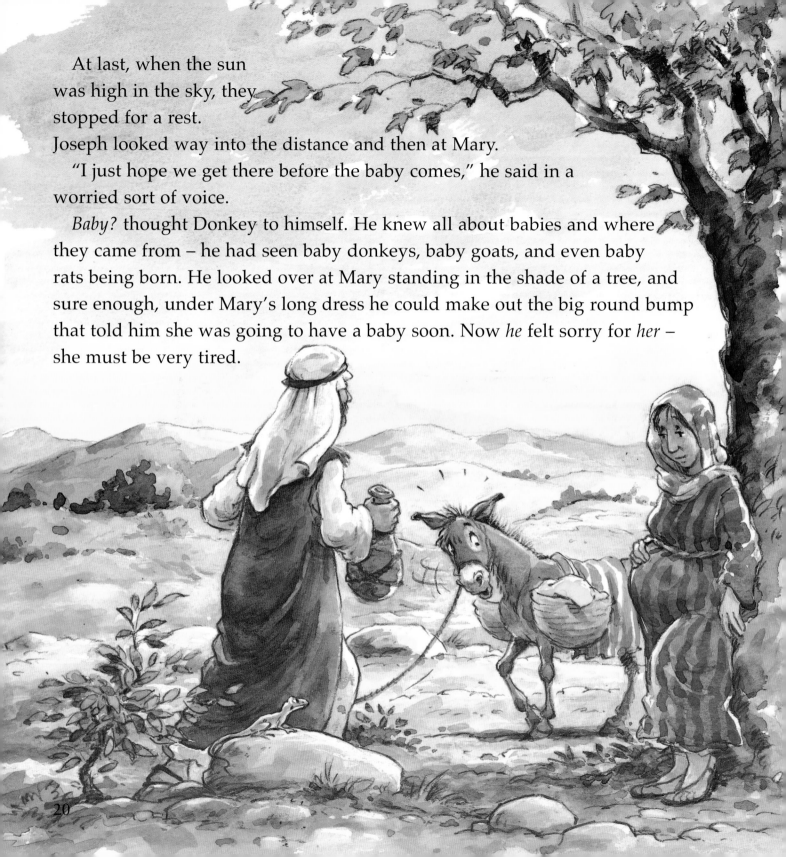

At last, when the sun was high in the sky, they stopped for a rest. Joseph looked way into the distance and then at Mary.

"I just hope we get there before the baby comes," he said in a worried sort of voice.

Baby? thought Donkey to himself. He knew all about babies and where they came from – he had seen baby donkeys, baby goats, and even baby rats being born. He looked over at Mary standing in the shade of a tree, and sure enough, under Mary's long dress he could make out the big round bump that told him she was going to have a baby soon. Now *he* felt sorry for *her* – she must be very tired.

20

So, when the sun began to sink down, late in the afternoon, and Joseph said it was time to get going, Donkey trotted over to Mary's side and nudged her arm gently. She looked down at him and he nudged her again.

"Are you trying to tell me something?" she laughed.

"I hope he's trying to tell you that he'll not be so stubborn this time," said Joseph.

So Mary climbed back onto Donkey and they set off once more.

At nightfall, Joseph rigged up a shelter with some of the blankets and Mary cooked a meal over a fire made of sticks she had gathered. When they had eaten, and Mary was cleaning the oil from the pan with her fingers, she suddenly got to her feet and came over to Donkey. She gently rubbed the rest of the oil into the sore patches on his skin. Donkey was amazed – no one had ever been kind to him before.

"Thank you for carrying me," she whispered.

And so it went on day after day – trudging along in the cooler times of the day and camping out in the evening under scrubby bushes, with Donkey tethered to a tree.

But one morning Donkey was awakened by shouting. Joseph was standing pointing at him crossly.

"It's empty!" he cried. "Empty! All those nuts and that bread –
what are we going to eat for the rest of the journey?"

"It was you, you greedy creature!" he cried. "You've had them…"

But Mary ran forward. "Don't be silly. Donkey was tied to that
tree all night. How could he have taken the food?"

Joseph wasn't listening – he was pacing about. "I don't
understand it – where's it all gone?" Then he muttered,
"I smell a rat."

Donkey suddenly pricked up his ears – why hadn't he thought of
that? *A rat!*

He looked about carefully and sure enough, there was Rat at the top of the other basket, lounging smugly on a fat bag of nuts.

"Don't you ever do that again!" Donkey snorted angrily.

Rat didn't move. "Why not?" he replied lazily. "You've changed sides. What have People ever done for you?"

Donkey fell silent.

Then, when Joseph had packed up their belongings, they set off on another long day's walk.

Mary climbed carefully onto Donkey's back.

"Do be patient with him," she said to Joseph. "We need him as much as he needs us."

This made Donkey feel very special indeed. *They needed him!*

On the morning of the seventh day Joseph was up and about even earlier than usual. He seemed worried.

"We've got to move fast if we're going to make it to Bethlehem by nightfall," he said to Mary.

The sun seemed hotter and the path rougher, but still they stumbled on, not even stopping for a rest in the middle of the day. As the sun began to sink behind the hills, Joseph tried to cheer Mary up.

"Not too far now – I'm sure if we just get up to the top of this hill…"

He ran a little way up the path.

"There's a short cut, a goat track we can take if…"

"Not if you've seen what I've seen," said a sharp little voice at Donkey's feet. Donkey looked down. There was Rat sunbathing on a low, flat rock.

"That path's crumbling away like nobody's business," murmured Rat.

"Come on!" called Joseph from the crest of the hill, "I can see Bethlehem from up here."

Donkey thought fast. He stood stock still and refused to budge. Mary tried to urge him on. She coaxed him, she warned him, but Donkey would not move.

"Come on!" shouted Joseph again.

Donkey let out a loud braying sound that echoed around the hillside. But still he did not move. Joseph ran back down the slope, and began to drag Donkey nearer and nearer to the edge of the cliff. Donkey dug his hooves into the stony path with all his might. Then…

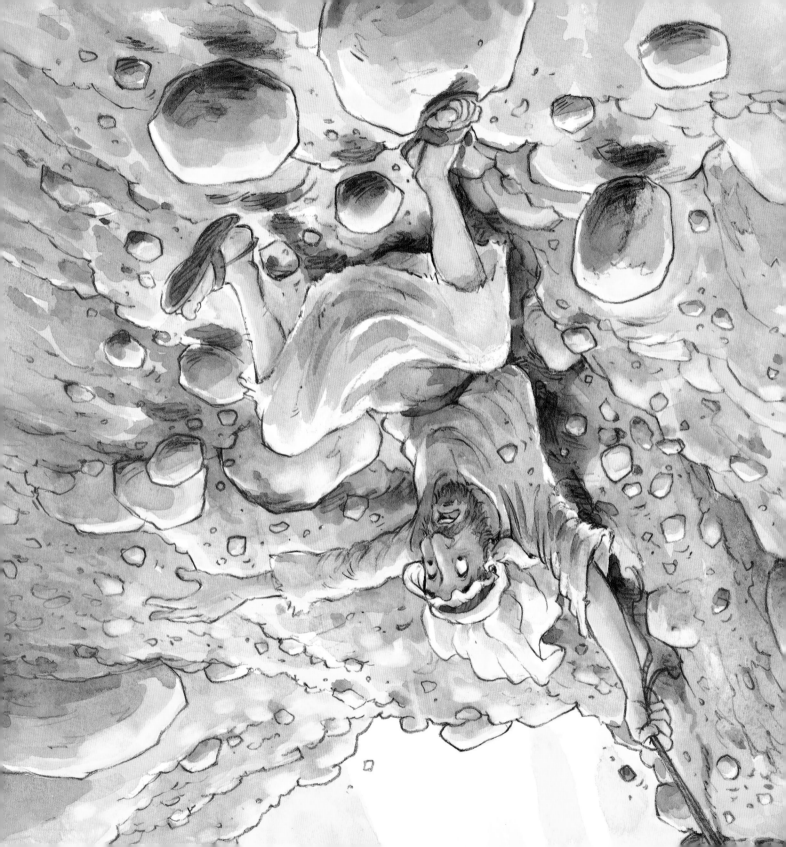

Joseph scrambled his way back up the rocks to where Mary and Donkey stood. He was trembling. He patted Donkey's head.

"If you hadn't been so pig-headed, that would've been all of us down there at the bottom of the cliff," he said wonderingly.

And as darkness fell, he put his arms around Mary and they sat on a rock to get over their fright.

Donkey stood in the dusk, his long rope trailing.

"You're not tied up now," said that sharp little voice again. "Here's your chance!"

Donkey looked down. He'd forgotten about Rat.

"If we make a run for it, you could be away before they even noticed," Rat went on.

"Why would I do that?" asked Donkey. He remembered Mary's words. "I need them as much as they need me," he said quietly.

Rat looked at him pityingly. "Then it's the parting of our ways," he replied. "I'm off. I can do without anyone else."

And he slunk off into the shadows without a backward glance.

29

It was very, very late and very, very dark when Donkey and Mary and Joseph finally dragged their tired feet into the little town of Bethlehem. They stumbled from door to door trying to find a place to stay. Donkey vaguely heard Joseph's voice pleading with a man. Then suddenly Donkey pricked up his ears. "…a nice warm stable…" the man was saying. To Donkey that sounded like paradise!

As Joseph gently led him down the dark alley to the back of the building, Donkey straightened up and tried to trot, to show Mary that everything would be all right when they got to the stable.

The big wooden door swung open and a single lantern lit up a great crowd of animals – goats and sheep, chickens, cows, and even rabbits.

Donkey pushed his way in.

"Come on, make some room here!" he commanded.

The animals shuffled their feet and stared at him.

"Why? Who are *you*?" they asked.

33

"Not for *me*. This is Mary – she's going to have a baby tonight."
"So? We have babies all the time," grumbled one of the rabbits.